The Legend of
Minnie's Pearl
and the Great Sweetwater Sea

ISBN 978-1533360946

First Edition 2016

rosevalleybooks@aol.com

For My Grandchildren
Taylor, Charlotte, Liam, and Devin

(The Children of the Future)

The Legend of Minnie's Pearl and the Great Sweetwater Sea

Chapter One

"Magic! Stay away from the fire!" Minnie cried. The little bear cub let out a squeal when Minnie scooped her up in her arms. She carried Magic back to the log she had been sitting on. "Fires are very bad!" Minnie told the little bear.

Minnie hugged Magic and kissed the top of her furry head. The little bear let out a sneeze. Her brother, Fuzz, who had been lying at Minnie's feet, jumped at the sound. He tried to crawl up Minnie's leg to be closer to his twin sister. Fuzz lost his balance and tumbled to the ground.

Minnie let out a sigh. "What am I going to do with you two? I can't imagine letting you wander in the woods on your own if you're afraid of a sneeze. What will happen if you hear an owl hoot or a cricket chirp?"

Minnie's grandfather, the chief of the Indian tribe, shook his head. "I would say it's a good idea not to spoil the bears! You wouldn't want one of them to sit in your lap when they are full grown. But right now they need a mother, and a mother's love to grow strong and healthy."

"Grandmother showed me how to make a special mash for the little bears to eat, Grandfather," Minnie said. "I tasted it." She made a funny face. She let out a big laugh when she saw her grandfather make a face too.

"You are a good mother to the little bears, Minnie. Too bad they don't have their own mother anymore. Someday you will be a good mother to your own children."

"I love them more than anything in the world." Minnie paused for a second thinking. "Well not more than my grandfather." Minnie gave grandfather a huge smile. Grandfather looked up into the night sky. The stars over his head were bright and shiny. The fire was warm and his granddaughter was near. Life was good, he thought. It had been a beautiful sunny day, but any time now the north winds could rise and bring the cold air that would sweep through their village. Everything could change in an instant. Grandfather wrapped his blanket around his shoulders. He shivered thinking of the freezing winds that would soon blow off the lake.

Fuzz and Magic cuddled close to Minnie's feet as she and her grandfather continued to watch the fire. The orange flames crackled and popped in the cool night air. The sound made her think of good things, like a walk in the woods when the leaves were falling or holding the tiny bears. It even made her think of her mother's sweet beautiful smile.

"Grandfather, please tell me a story," Minnie pleaded.

Grandfather pulled his blanket a little tighter around his shoulders. "Do you want me to tell you the story of how I got the grumpy old snapping turtle to behave? Or how about when I taught Mister Frog to leap higher than the trees? Maybe the one where Nana Bozo chased me through the woods and I ran into Elk Woman, knocking her into the stream? Did I ever tell you Elk Woman was carried ten miles into the lake before she was able to swim home again?"

"I think I would like a story about the First Bear, Grandfather," Minnie said.

"Ah the First Bear." Grandfather took a deep breath. "Well let's see. Did you know the First Bear is not black like your two little friends there. The First Bear is pure white like the Great White Trilliums that bloom on the floor of the forest. Did you know that when someone is sick the first bear can hug that person and make them well again?"

Minnie nodded. "You told me about the

First Bear when I was little. I just can't believe some bears are pure white!"

Grandfather grinned. "I did see the First Bear once. She definitely is a beauty. I saw her in the woods one night just after you were born. She was collecting star dust that had fallen to the earth to take back with her to her cave in the heavens. She uses it to get little children to sleep."

After Grandfather was finished telling another story of the First Bear, he turned to Minnie and said. "It's time for bed now."

Minnie gave a sad nod. "I wonder if the First Bear knows about the little cubs and how you found them?"

Grandfather nodded. "She's the one who led me to them. I found them lying beside their mother after she fell out of the tree."

Minnie frowned. "It's so sad to think their mother is gone to the heavens. But they have me now. I will always look after them."

"I'm sure you'll be a very good mother to the little bears," her grandfather said, motioning to her wigwam." Now it's time to go to bed. Good night Minnie." "Good night, grandfather," Minnie said, getting up from the log. The little bears scrambled to their feet and followed her as she turned to leave.

Chapter Two

"Good morning Fuzz!" Minnie sat down on the floor of the wigwam and kissed the top of the little bear's head. She did the same to Magic. "Good morning, Magic!" she exclaimed.

Magic's little tongue popped out of her mouth. It felt rough and ticklish against Minnie's cheek as the young bear returned the kiss.

Minnie walked over to the door of her little home in the woods and peered out. Almost all the homes or wigwams in the village where the Native Americans lived were like hers, except for one very long one where the elders of the tribe would meet. This much larger wigwam was called a lodge.

The wigwams were made up of green saplings and branches that were tied together and covered with birch bark, animal hide, and cloth. In Minnie's village the wigwams stood together in a circle on the edge of the woods near the big lake.

From the door of the wigwam Minnie could see the big lake. It was calm today. The sky overhead was clear and bright blue. She could see the sun was shining! When she heard birds chirping in the oak trees overhead, Minnie smiled and stretched. The birds singing always made her feel so happy inside!

Minnie found her buckskin tunic and got dressed. Afterwards she sat on the floor of the wigwam and slipped on her leather moccasins while the little bears played around her. When Minnie stood up, Fuzz let out a squeal. She'd almost stepped on his toes! "I am so sorry, Fuzz!" Minnie exclaimed.

Minnie sat down again and hugged Fuzz for several moments trying to calm the agitated little bear. Within moments Magic wanted to be hugged too.

When Fuzz and Magic were both quiet and happy, Minnie looked around the wigwam. "What should we do today?" she asked herself.

Minnie grinned. Of course! She would teach the bears how to fish.

Minnie found her spear and the basket her mother had made for her out of reeds. She had given it to Minnie for her birthday. Fuzz and Magic sniffed at the basket, wondering what it was.

Minnie tied the basket on her shoulders, wearing it like a back pack. Smiling happily, she headed out the door with the little cubs trailing after her.

Minnie was grinning from ear to ear as she walked down the path to the stream. Oh how she loved to fish! She began to sing a song of thanksgiving to the forest and the river as she walked along.

After a time, Minnie came across a huge tree lying across the trail. She knew it had fallen down in a storm. She stopped and waited by the tree for the young bears to catch up with her. Then she crawled over the tree and stood on the other side watching as the cubs scrambled over the log themselves, then tumbled to the ground at her feet.

Just then Minnie heard a loud burp. She was certain it came from the swamp nearby. She looked around expectantly. Sometimes her brother would hide in the bushes and make animal sounds to trick her. Minnie knew Flying Turtle liked to imitate the coyotes and wolves that lived in the big woods. But most of all Flying Turtle loved to imitate the frogs.

Once again, Minnie heard a loud burp coming from the swamp. She finally let out a laugh. Of course, it was only a frog!

Minnie shook her head. She thought of the funny faces Flying Turtle always made when he imitated the frogs. Her big brother looked especially silly when he puffed his cheeks out to look like one of them.

Minnie was very grateful her brother hadn't put any baby garter snakes in her moccasins lately. The tiny snakes made her squeal when she slipped the shoes on her feet and felt the little snakes wiggle around her toes.

Come to think of it, Minnie thought, she hadn't found a pine cone in her bed in weeks. Flying Turtle loved to hide them between her blankets. He would pretend to be innocent when she sat down on top of them and they made her jump and squeal. Her mother would shoo her brother out of the wigwam shaking her head.

The last thing she found in her bed that her brother had put there wasn't a pine cone at all. One night when she pulled back her blankets she saw two little brown eyes blinking up at her. That evening she'd taken the little toad outside and set it down in a safe place under a nearby tree where it happily hopped away.

Flying Turtle was definitely a prankster, Minnie thought. But she knew her brother had a good heart. When someone was being bullied Flying Turtle always made sure they knew he was there to help.

When Minnie finally got to the stream, she found her favorite spot. For several moments she looked down at her reflection in the water. Two very large dark eyes stared back at her. At first she didn't recognize herself. Her long coarse black hair, which was usually gathered in braids on either side of her head, now hung loose over her shoulders. It looked much longer. It also looked like she had grown taller.

Minnie gazed at her reflection, finally making a face at herself. She thought of the silly faces her brother always made when he imitated animals. Minnie puffed

her cheeks out. She crossed her eyes. She
even stuck out her tongue for a moment.
Then she spun around, trying to see her
whole body in the water.

Minnie knew she looked like her mother, Laughing Deer, except she was much smaller. Everyone loved her mother's smile, especially her father and grandfather.

Minnie realized it had been a whole month since she had gone fishing with Grandfather. She missed the afternoons they spent talking while they fished.

Time was flying by, Minnie thought. Her mother once told her time was like a slimy fish that was hard to hold. And that she must spend her time wisely.

She decided long ago fishing was a good thing to spend time on. Another thing she liked to spend time on was carving wood.

Her father had taught her how to carve little beads that looked liked animals that she would make into necklaces for herself or for her friends in the village.

Her grandfather had taught her how to carve a flute out of a piece of pine. And her mother had taught her how to play music on the flute. Minnie smiled remembering the many times she had played the flute for her family when they sat around the fire talking in the evening.

She loved to fill the air with music when the day was dark and sombre and clouds covered the sky, then everything would seem beautiful again in spite of the darkness.

Minnie gazed at the little cubs who had gone down to the stream to play. The cubs looked so sweet and innocent as they poked around in the water. She knew one day they would be full grown bears. They would need to return to the forest. Minnie shook her head. She quickly put the sad thought away.

Minnie finally gave a smile, deciding nothing would take her happiness from her today. Nothing!

Suddenly a fish jumped in front of Minnie. She could see two more fish at the bottom of the stream near a pile of rocks. Minnie felt cold water splash against her face. She could now see more fish gathering at the bottom of the stream near the rock pile.

Minnie quickly stepped into the water with her spear. Within seconds another trout leapt into the air, smacking into the water near her with a loud plop.

Just at that moment, she heard one of the little bears let out a squeal.

Fuzz and Magic scurried onto the shore in a panic. Minnie shook her head when she realized the little cubs had been frightened by the jumping fish!

"Bears afraid of fish! How silly!" Minnie exclaimed.

She gazed at Fuzz who was now panting very hard. He looked so frightened that she walked over to him. She tried to scoop him up into her arms.

Fuzz was certainly getting heavy, Minnie thought as she kissed the top of his head. He was also dripping wet!

"Yuck," Minnie cried when she realized her mistake. Minnie quickly put Fuzz down. She gazed at the front of her tunic. It was now wet and slimy!

Minnie looked around for Magic. Where was she?

In that instant, she spotted a man with thick black hair on his face watching her from across the stream! For a second Minnie was too frightened to move.

The man was close enough that she could see his blue eyes when he poked his head out to look at her from behind a tree.

Her native people who had lived in the woods for as long as anyone could remember all had very dark eyes! This human was different not like her family at all.

Besides the color of his eyes, he had long black hair on his head. He also had black hair covering his face and chin. In fact, he looked just like a bear! Then Minnie heard him sneeze. "Achoo!" The sound rang out from across the stream and echoed in the woods. He was a man alright, unlike any man she had ever seen before!

Minnie ran home as fast as she could with Fuzz and Magic trying to keep up.

She knew she must tell her grandfather about the strange man. Her grandfather would need to know about him and if he was dangerous.

Chapter Three

"It was like Manitou-Magic!" Minnie exclaimed when she told her grandfather about the man she had seen standing behind the trees at the stream. "He looked just like a bear. I'm sure he was part man and part bear!"

Grandfather's face grew sad, "More like him will come," he said, shaking his head. "Minnie, if he is truly a man, he will bring others. We have reason to be concerned."

"But why grandfather?"

Grandfather looked up into the dark sky overhead. He saw by reading the stars that a great number of *manitous* surrounded his granddaughter this night. They were very good omens.

Grandfather finally looked at Minnie with sparkling eyes. She looked so small sitting by the crackling fire with the tiny bear cubs nestled around her feet, but

Grandfather knew Minnie's heart was brave.

"Only those who have the burning light in their hearts can attempt to change what is written," her grandfather said. "Minnie you have this light in your heart. Use it well to bring healing to the earth."

Minnie was confused "Grandfather, what do you mean?" she asked. "Why does the earth need to be healed?"

Grandfather looked up at the sky again and thoughtfully nodded. He brushed a tear away from his eye when he looked at his granddaughter once more. "The stars tell me our world is about to change. And it will be you, little one, who will bring a great understanding to the earth.

"Me? I really don't understand what you mean, Grandfather. What can I do?" Minnie asked.

The flames of the fire grew smaller and smaller while they talked. "I am just a small child," she finally added with a sigh. Minnie felt Fuzz's little tongue lick her fingers and she gave a sad smile.

"The Great Spirit will show you the answer, Minnie," her grandfather told her.

Minnie was frightened and confused by her grandfather's words. Were they all in danger because of the man she had seen?

That night Minnie had a very strange dream. It was stranger than any dream she had ever dreamt before. Even though she was frightened, a voice inside Minnie told her she must travel bravely in this land of dreams to see everything and remember it all.

In her dream Minnie saw that the big lake had turned a horrible brown. There were dead fish lying along the shore as she walked along the beach. She could actually smell the fish. She wrinkled her nose at the awful smell.

In one of the trees above her she could see an eagle sitting on a branch. The great bird spread its wings. It soared high into the sky. Then it began to fall. Minnie couldn't bear to watch as the eagle began to plummet to the earth. She turned her head away at the last second, but couldn't help but hear the loud thump when it hit the ground. Tears gathered in Minnie's eyes.

The saddest part of the dream was when the strange men appeared on the shore of the big lake. Some of them had blue eyes like the bear-man she had spotted in the woods. They came on large boats with huge white sails that caught the air and reminded her of bird wings. Their boats were much larger than the birch bark canoes her people used on the rivers and streams.

When the men got out of their boats and marched into the forests, Minnie heard the sound of chopping and hammering.

Still dreaming, Minnie watched as the men returned to the boats. She let out a horrible cry in her sleep when she realized there were now row upon row of stumps where the proud trees had once stood.

The sad looking brown stumps covered the landscape for as far as her eyes could see and then some. The entire forest had disappeared!

Minnie let out a second, louder, cry in her sleep. Only this time it was more urgent. Minnie's cry woke up her brother and mother and the two little bears that slept beside her. Flying Turtle leapt out of his bed and ran to her. He shook Minnie's shoulders to wake her up. Fuzz and Magic helped to wake her by licking her face. When Minnie finally opened her eyes her mother was standing over them all. Laughing Deer looked very concerned.

Minnie sat up and looked around the wigwam. She rubbed her eyes. Then she blinked several times.

"It was only a dream," Laughing Deer said.

"But it was so real," Minnie said. Minnie finally gave a small smile when Flying Turtle let out a huge burp to make her laugh. And for good measure he gave several owl hoots to get her to giggle.

Minnie's mother shook her head. She shooed Flying Turtle out of the lodge.

Minnie got dressed and ran to the big lodge where her grandfather, the chief of their tribe, had gathered with the elders. Grandfather was sitting by the fire wearing his head dress. When he saw Minnie he motioned to her to sit down next to him. Minnie then told them all about her dream.

Her grandfather, whose native name actually was Proud Eagle, looked very concerned. "It's a dream of the future," he explained. "I have had dreams of this myself."

"What will our tribe do if all the trees are chopped down?" Minnie asked the elders, thinking of Fuzz and Magic. "The little bears will not have a home in the forest if all the trees are gone. Where will they play? Where will they raise their families? And what will everyone eat if all the fish die because of brown waters," she asked.

Then Minnie thought of the children in her tribe. "What will the children do?" she asked them. "They will not have their beautiful homes by the big lake without all the trees. It will be very ugly and sad."

The elders could only shake their heads. They didn't have an answer for Minnie. None of them could imagine a world without the trees. None of them could imagine a world without a beautiful blue big lake nearby filled with crystal clear water. They all looked very sad, indeed.

Chapter Four

The next day, Minnie sat on a small log by the stream at her favorite fishing spot. The only thing she felt like doing was crying. Tears began to roll down Minnie's cheeks and onto the ground making a small puddle. She could see mud was beginning to form at her feet.

Fuzz and Magic played in the puddle. The two little bears got dirtier and dirtier as they tumbled around in the dirty water. The cubs only got happier and happier as more and more tears poured from Minnie's eyes making the puddle larger and larger.

Magic snorted. Water got into her nose when she sniffed around the edges of the puddle. It made Minnie smile for just a moment. Then she went back to crying.

The children in her tribe were confused and worried when they saw Minnie crying. What was wrong with her, they wondered?

One of the braves, an older boy, who liked to tease everyone, made up a new name for her.

"Minnie Boo Hoo, if you don't stop crying you will flood the whole wide world with your tears!" Cawing Crow, teased. "We will have to use canoes just to get from wigwam to wigwam!"

It certainly didn't feel good to be called names, Minnie thought. But she couldn't help how she felt. It hurt to think of what the future would be like in their village without all the beautiful trees surrounding them.

Minnie looked up into the sky and remembered what grandfather had told her. She began to sing a song to the Great Spirit hoping he would come.

"Minnie, why do you mourn so?" asked the Great Spirit after hearing her song. "No one has died. Your tears are making your tribe very unhappy and confused."

"I'm afraid of what I see in the future, Great Spirit." Minnie said.

"What are you afraid of, little Minnie?" asked the Great Spirit. "What is wrong?"

"I have seen some very troubling things, Great Spirit." Minnie said. "I know more men like the bear-man will come to our beautiful land. They will cut down many of the trees. I'm afraid for all the animals and children. Where will they live when the forests are gone? Why must this happen?"

"Soothe your heart, my child," said the Great Spirit.

Suddenly Minnie felt a gentle breeze caress her arm. A warm tingle spread through her body and she no longer felt like crying.

"Thank you, Great Spirit," Minnie said.

That night Minnie had another dream. She knew it was a very special dream the Great Spirit had sent her.

In this dream, she was walking along in a field of pine stumps with Fuzz and Magic. She knew she had cried away all of her tears at the sight of the ruined trees in her last dream. *In this dream,* she only had one small tear left to shed. She felt it roll down her face. She watched as it spilled onto the parched earth at her toes.

Minnie looked down for several moments unable to move. She saw a tiny plant sprout out of the dirt! Then a small flower began to bloom on the plant. Minnie watched in amazement as the flower grew larger and larger. Then the petals on the plant slowly opened before her eyes.

Minnie blinked several times, not believing what she saw. Cradled within the little white flower was a tiny sleeping baby!

Minnie was mesmerized as she watched the tiny baby move about in its sleep.

The baby finally yawned and stretched in front of her, then ever so slowly opened its tiny clenched fist. She could see that it was holding something.

Waking up before she could tell what the baby held, Minnie surprised herself. She already knew what it was! It was a tiny pearl!

She had once found a pearl in one of the half opened shells on the shore while she had been walking along the beach near the great dune of the Sleeping Bear with her grandfather. That same afternoon Grandfather had told her the story of the Sleeping Mother Bear and her cubs.

Minnie tried hard to remember all of the details of the story her grandfather had told her. She remembered that the Great Mother Bear and her two little cubs had tried to flee a forest fire by swimming across the big lake. When they were halfway across the water the two little cubs become very tired. Mother Bear tried hard to encourage them to stay behind her, but when she looked back they were gone. They had become too tired to keep up with her and sank beneath the waves.

Mother Bear reached the shore safely. She was filled with great sadness at the loss of her precious little cubs. She fell into a very deep sleep on the beach, overlooking the spot where her cubs had vanished. To comfort Mother Bear, the Great Spirit covered her with a blanket of sand. Grandfather said she was now one of the giant dunes that Minnie saw on the shore.

The next night Minnie herself fell into a deep sleep after playing her flute. She found herself in another dream. *In this dream* she was walking along the shore of the big lake again. When she realized she was near the great dune of the Sleeping Mother Bear she began to smile. Somehow she knew something wonderful was about to happen.

In the dream Minnie felt the warm sun on her back. She also heard water lapping gently on the beach while sea gulls called from overhead. The familiar sounds were soothing and sweet. She knew the dream the Great Spirit had given her was meant to heal her sadness.

In the distance Minnie heard someone singing. She also saw two bears cubs who were not Fuzz and Magic standing on the shore near the great dunes.

Minnie knew The Great Mother Bear had awakened from her sleep and was singing a beautiful song to her cubs!

Minnie could see the cubs were swaying from side to side while they listened intently to their mother's voice.

Awaken, Oh, My Children,

Awaken from your slumber,

Let your eyes be clear and bright

For sand no longer blinds us

And confuses our direction.

The way is Clear, My children,

Cast away the Swirling Sands from

Your eyes and know

The true direction

By following those

Footprints in the sand

Before you

Which lead into the Land of Light.

When Minnie woke up the next morning she ran to tell grandfather about the beautiful dream she had that night. She felt happy and peaceful.

Chapter Five

The very next day, instead of sitting by the river crying again, Minnie spent the afternoon working. She began to fashion a figure out of a piece of white pine like her father had taught her. This time, she didn't make a carving of a bird or a flute, but instead worked on a replica of the little child she had seen in her dream, sleeping peacefully in the petals of the flower.

The sleeping baby's face became more and more beautiful as Minnie worked — word of its astonishing beauty brought all of the children in the tribe to see it. They stood around Minnie and watched as she crafted the carving. Flying Turtle and Cawing Crow were among them. The children were all amazed at Minnie's talent.

Curious about what Minnie was doing, the tribal elders came to see the carving They too were astounded at what she had fashioned out of the piece of pine.

The carving actually looked like a real

flesh-and-blood baby. The little doll was so lifelike it could be mistaken for a real papoose, yet it was only a piece of wood.

"Who is this sleeping child?" one of the tribal elders asked, Minnie.

Minnie did not have a name, but she knew in her heart who it was! She knew it was a *child of the future*! Minnie knew it was a *child* who would one day awaken from its sleep and find a way to save the big lake from the sour brown waters she had seen in her dream. She knew the child would stop the forests from disappearing!

Minnie somehow knew that the pearl in the baby's hand would one day be planted into the hearts of future children all over the world and it would help them to grow up to love and protect the earth!

Minnie was overwhelmed with happiness as she worked on her carving of the beautiful sleeping baby. Everyone in the tribe was relieved that Minnie had stopped crying.

Minnie began to sing a joyful song to the Great Spirit hoping he would come so she could thank him.

"Someday all of the children in the future will know of you, Minnie," the Great Spirit told her, "because you truly love them. The children of the future will see your bright and shining light across the bridge of time. I can't tell you how, but it will happen."

"The many tears you have shed for the forests and the rivers and the sea will sweeten the sour brown waters of the future! I promise you that!" The Great Spirit said. "When you think you are too small to make a difference, little one, always remember this, and tell all the children too, that small things can do many things large things cannot!"

A wondrous wind blew up just then. The sun went down and the night sky was filled with an ocean of glittering stars overhead. Minnie could see beautiful pictures of many different kinds of animals outlined with stars in the darkness above her. She was reminded of the many woodland creatures that lived in the forests near her home.

Suddenly, a firefly landed on Minnie's arm. Its tiny twinkle delighted her. It was so small and delicate, yet it sparkled radiantly in the dark night like a little jewel, making her break into a huge smile. "No tears, no tears." Minnie whispered to herself. She only wanted to smile with happiness when the firefly landed on her nose.

"The children of the future will catch the light of love that is in you right now Minnie, and will pass it on to each other with their own twinkling eyes," the Great Spirit said.

Minnie crossed her eyes to see the firefly sitting on her nose.

The Great Spirit began to laugh at how

silly she looked. His playful laugh rolled across the sky like rumbling thunder just before a spring rain.

Minnie couldn't help but join him. Her own laugh tinkled in the night like a joyous bell resounding in the darkness.

"*Minnie Ha Ha,* you will flood the whole wide world with your joy!" Cawing Crow called out.

Minnie suddenly realized that Cawing Crow had given her a new name. It was one that she actually liked!

"Like that firefly your joy will go from heart to heart like a tiny spark. It will awaken many minds to the wonders of love," the Great Spirit explained. "Your spark of hope will heal the world, Minnie. Your tears for the earth, and the animals, and the dear children, will be the salt that gives sweetness to the seas once again!"

Minnie was overwhelmed by what the Great Spirit said. Once again she began to laugh. Her laughter filled the air around her making all the children in the tribe start laughing too!

After what the Great Spirit told her, Minnie felt like a giant! Little Minnie who always felt so small, now felt like the Great Mother Bear awakening to protect her precious cubs!

With a river of happiness flowing through her, Minnie thought of the First Bear of Creation hugging the earth to her body to heal it. Most of all she thought of all the good things that would happen because of the children who would one day awaken and grow up to love and protect the earth.

Fuzz and Magic came to sit at Minnie's feet. Magic looked up at her with big questioning brown eyes while Fuzz tried to crawl into her lap. She scooped the little bear into her arms and hugged him close. Minnie noticed grandfather was now standing in the crowd with the elders wearing his beautiful headdress. It was the one he only wore for the most special of special occasions. Minnie realized he had put it on just for her!

Denise Coughlin

What are things we can do to protect our water, our air, our trees?

What are some things that pollute our streams?

What are toxins?

What type of toxins can we find in water?

What type of toxins can we find in the air and can toxins make us sick?

Author Biography

Denise Coughlin loves writing stories for children! She is an author, an artist and a public speaker. She lives in the beautiful state of Michigan with her husband Ken. Denise has been writing stories since she was a little girl. She has written several books for children and adults.

For information on author visits for children or workshops for writers please contact her via email. Please specify author presentations.

Acknowledgements

Cover design by Carl Virgilio

Cover Art courtesy of Candice Greive

Illustrations by Gail Borowski

Made in the USA
Columbia, SC
07 December 2017